"You are that which you
seek."

[signature]

Ivory Leonard IV
Self Published
sankofa1619.production@gmail.com
Website: www.sankofa1619.com

Printed by Amazon, in the United States of America.
First printing Edition 2020.

Illustrations by Saeed Briscoe.
Saeedsvpllc@gmail.com
SaeedsVP.net

3

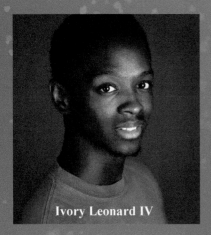

Ivory Leonard IV

CEO | Founder of Sankofa1619, LLC
Website: www.sankofa1619.com

About the Author

I remember reading books that expanded my imagination as a child. There's something quite magical about children's books. It gives children the ability to recondition their minds and see what is possible- at least- that's what it did for me.

As a storyteller, words have been important to Black individuals to continue our heritage. As an extension of Sankofa1619, LLC., I created this series of books to re-claim our past, re-define how we are defined, and re-connect to our truth.

As CEO and Founder of Sankofa1619, LLC., I am beyond grateful to share this work that I've learned through personal experience, research, and imagination. With hopes of Black and Brown children seeing themselves in a light that is accessible from within, through iconography, mysticism, and connection to ancestry - may this work be transformative and allow us to become aware of what a world would be without colonialism. As the Cradle of Civilization and Originators of humanity, this information is not new, nor fictional, this is what we are.

I want to thank my mom Dawn Bristow, sister Ebony Leonard, aunt Stacey Williams, mentor Patdro Harris, godmother Denise A. Davis, and my dear friends for their consistent encouragement. More importantly, this is for my ancestors who fought and continue to fight for liberation and equality. I can't thank you enough.

With hopes of a better world!

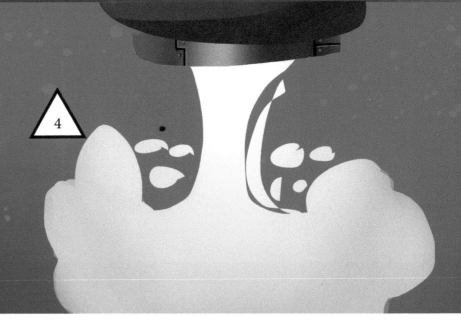

4

Dedicated to my sister
Ivy Leonard

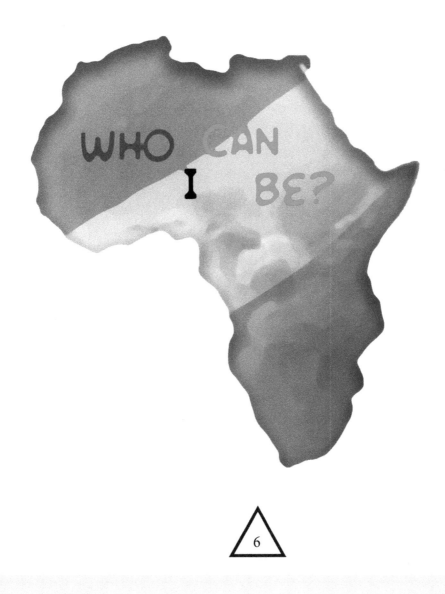

We invite you to explore this world with a concluding activity on page: # 26

I want to be a firefighter and
save kittens from a tree.

Or fight crime like an officer who
protects kids like me.

Maybe, a pilot who can see a bird soar high in the sky.

Or a doctor who gives lollipops so kids don't cry.

Oh I wonder, I wonder, who can I be?

How about a teacher who saves the world?

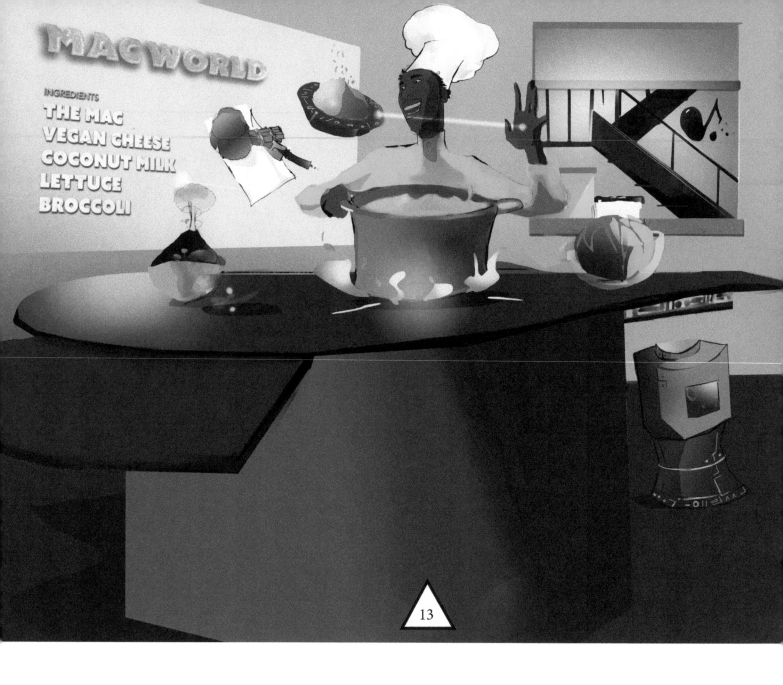

Or maybe a chef who creates Macworld?

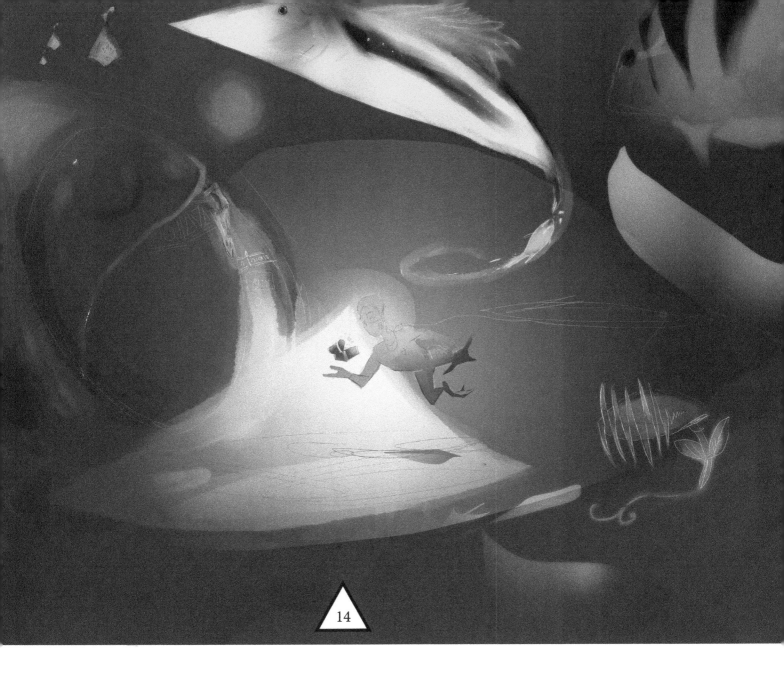

Dive deep in the ocean to a world in the sea.

Oh I wonder, I wonder, who can I be?

I can plan a big party so kids can have a ball.
Throw candy in the air so we can have it all!

I just want to have fun how can you disagree?

Oh I wonder, I wonder, who can I be?

Then one day my mom said to me,
"Son, you can be anything you want to be."

"You're already the sun, the moon, even the trees.
Just never allow anyone to tell you who to be."

I like that. I like that very much. Well, maybe not a tree.
I just want to be me.

If that's an actor, a lawyer, dancer, or singer.
Or janitor, inventor, or curator you see.
These are only jobs, just jobs, not me.

Because the only thing that will make me happy...
Is me!

To be continued...

(Flip page for activity.)

Congratulations!

Treasure Hunt

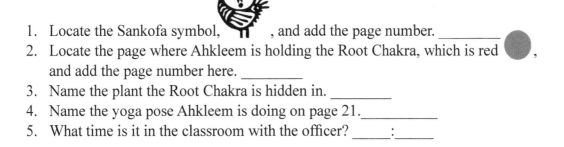

1. Locate the Sankofa symbol, , and add the page number. _____
2. Locate the page where Ahkleem is holding the Root Chakra, which is red ⬤ , and add the page number here. _____
3. Name the plant the Root Chakra is hidden in. _____
4. Name the yoga pose Ahkleem is doing on page 21._____
5. What time is it in the classroom with the officer? _____:_____

Upon completion, follow, tag, and repost @sankofa1619 on Instagram with your answers. First 50 with the correct answers will be shared.

△
26

Sankofa - to go back and get what is lost.

Root Chakra - located at the base of the spine. Associated with the color red. Includes basic needs; such as: food, water, shelter, safety, as well as connection, strength, and fearlessness.